Love Anonymous

Fred Adage

Love Anonymous
by Fred Adage

Fred Adage is a pseudonym.
The true author wishes to remain anonymous.

ISBN 978-1-77335-131-5

This is a work of fiction. Names, characters, businesses,
places, events and incidents are products of the author's
imagination. Any resemblance to actual persons, living or
dead, or actual events, is purely coincidental.

Magdalene Press, 2019
Dorval, Quebec

Prologue

I am surprised that there are so many people here. Astrid recommended it. She said I would never recover, be well again, from that ordeal I just went through. She packed her bags and put them on the bed. But I am not a cheater, I said. Nothing happened. We just talked, and stuff. Just talked. And yet, here I am, ready for my turn. There isn't really much talking to do. It was short, but it left me changed. Different. Not sure what to make of it. It makes no sense. I am here so that Astrid does not leave me. She packed her bags, after all. And she smells like fish. That part I cannot tell. The rest I will. The sexual details I will omit. This place is, after all, the most nonsensical thing I ever heard: Love Anonymous. Who ever heard of such a thing? A fabrication to acknowledge that which is weak. And yet here I am. For Astrid. Who smells like fish.

1

My name is Fred, and I am a coward.

I have other qualities, but I am undeniably a coward. Sometimes I tell myself maybe I'm not a coward. Maybe I'm just smart and logical and refuse to be swayed by female wiles like a nonsensical fool. See, I pride myself on being logical. Before a decision is made, one has to think about it for a long time. One has to know for sure that it's right. One cannot simply follow like a puppy because a woman is gorgeous and trying to convince him to do something that makes no sense.

Her name is May. She calls herself Mayday. I tried to call her by her real name many times, but she insists I call her Mayday. I asked to see her driver's license. I feel the need to find things out. She showed it to me, and it says May. But that is the least of my worries right now.

She wants me to marry her and have a baby with her, and I've only known her three years. Yes, we fell madly in love. But all this could very well be an illusion, a trick of the mind. What is love, after all, if not a trick of the mind? Yes, I feel it, I know, many people have felt it. But it's nonsense. I cannot base a decision on nonsense—though I do feel something beyond my control.

Mayday says she is my soul mate, that since the very beginning she's felt compelled to follow me around, that she cannot say no to me even when she normally would to anyone else. She says that there is a special energy, one very unique and that our souls know each other.

I tell her a soul doesn't even exist. It is a figment of the imagination. Humans have created it so as to justify God. That too is a story. In fact it is the biggest lie of all.

Mayday says I have no faith, and because I have no faith I have fear, fear of doing anything. She says to close my eyes and feel her soul—that if love exists, which it does because I feel it for her, then a soul and God exist. She says I cannot touch God just like I cannot touch love. If love exists, then God exists.

She says thousands of years from now people will write thousands of books trying to prove that love does not exist, and yet others will say—just like they now say about God—"but I feel it. I feel love. How can you tell me it does not exist?"

Mayday is a fervent believer in God. She is the opposite of me and does not make sense, and yet I love her. I do not trust her entirely, but I love her. Some May argue that this is passion, but it feels like love.

Regardless, I do not plan on making any kind of move forward until I know for sure what this is.

Mayday says I should leave my girlfriend of eight years and just have faith in the power of love. I say I must find out first. She says the boat is sailing, will sail without me. I say I must find out. She says I am a coward.

I say she is a maneater. She chews on men and spits them out. She says she is only looking for a soul mate. She has found love many times before and that was never enough. She wants a soul mate to rock her soul. She calls it the creative kind of love—soul love—one that will recreate itself with each passing moment. Regular love, as most people have it, just fades and dies and people end up bored with one another. She says regular love just evolves into deep friendship and camaraderie, and this isn't enough for her. The only kind that will stand the test of time is one that will change with the moments, just like the universe; no two seconds are the same. Creative love, she says, is like universal creation. I often do not understand what she means.

"So what do you want?" I ask her for the hundredth time.

"Nothing, I want nothing from you."

"Then why are you here again?"

"Because I want to be."

I have asked her the same question many times. "I want your soul on a platter," she says flippantly after a few moments of silence.

"What does that mean?"

"Nothing."

"What does that mean, my soul on a platter?"

"Nothing, it just means I want to be close to you."

"What are you doing to me?"

"Nothing."

I should have listened more carefully to her. I should have known she was too smart to misuse words. No "thing" would suffice for her. She was looking for a soul. And she wanted me to hand it over on a silver platter.

2

My name is Fred, and I am a Savior.

I saved someone three years ago. That's what Mayday said turned her on to me.

I walked into a café she frequented. I had seen a sign outside advertising the writing event and decided to go in though I disliked crowds. I had been there before. I love mathematics and wanted to put together a mathematics book. I would build it meticulously. It would be perfect.

I entered the café and took a seat near the door.

Mayday, wearing a frilly, pink gypsy skirt, got up and headed toward the manager of the café. "I'd like to have a permanent table where I can give advice," she said confidently. Her English gave away her French roots yet was immaculate. "It would draw crowds," she continued, looking at me for signs of agreement. She was a regular customer. I had seen her before. She often had groups of people around her, laughing, joking. She was friendly and flirtatious, playing with her hair or rocking where she stood were like breathing to her. She couldn't risk another relationship in this place. Once had been a bust, and that was it. She was here only for inspiration and entertainment. And perhaps she could create a few things in the process. It was creating that kept her alive. What it was didn't matter. She always had to make something from nothing—give life to something that hadn't been before.

"I love to give advice, and it would add some flavor to this place." She looked nervous by the manager's non-responsiveness. For whatever reason, he seemed frozen in time.

At last he said, barely audible, "Well...."

She stared and waited.

"Why don't you set up a booth outside?" I got up from my seat and began walking toward her.

"Hmmm...I don't know. Wouldn't I need a permit from the city?" she said turning to me, looking somewhat stunned.

"Yes, but it isn't difficult to get. You can apply for it at the local city hall. I'm sure they'll give it to you."

"Hmmm...okay." She appeared slightly embarrassed by the manager's unspoken refusal. She had dared, and she had failed.

The manager turned his head toward the middle of the room and rolled his eyes. Someone was standing on a chair and shouting with his arms extended.

"Hello, everyone! I am Ian Fane, and I am here today to offer my help. I will help you with anything and everything. You just ask. I will offer my services to the best of my abilities and will go to the ends of the earth to help you—”

Everyone in the room laughed. It sounded like grunting animals ready for a feast. The smell of a victim was in the air.

I turned and began walking towards Ian Fane.

“Wait, what are you doing?” started Mayday, but she was too slow. I was already by Ian’s side.

I felt everyone watching me, especially her. The pack in the room was getting ready for the kill. The energy in the air was foaming. Mayday said later she could feel it tingling her skin. She knew what was going to happen. She had seen it before. It was something about writer-wannabes. The frustrated anger they harbored. They would surely draw blood again.

“So, master genius,” began Siva, a regular and moderately successful author. “What are you going to do for us exactly? Are you going to hold our hand as we write?”

The group laughed like a bomb. It was getting loud.

"I want to help," said Ian. "I want to help all of you. Anything you need. I am at your service."

"Why don't you go feign some phone calls for me, Fane! And don't be profane about it!" shouted Amba, sitting nearest to Ian.

The manager said nothing.

Ian did not budge. He stood there with a confused and hurt look on his face.

"Heya, Ian boy, why don't you write a work of art for me? What exactly have you written anyway that makes you so qualified to help us struggling authors?" said Manuel, another regular.

Ian just stood. His head leaned slightly to his right. He faced the door then looked up at the ceiling.

"I would like some help, sir," said Mayday, sprinting toward him. "I've been looking for inspiration for a new book. I really don't know what to write about. I wrote a book called Soul Pain Be

Gone, and now I'm stuck. For the life of me, I don't know what to write about next."

Ian gazed at her for a second then slowly got off the chair and walked to his table without turning once.

"Ian, my friend," I blurted, "since the beginning of time, man has been fighting man. I have been wondering all my life: How can MAN (including WOMAN) end all conflict immediately and unconditionally?

"I need some answers regarding humankind. Is man evil? Is there any hope for man? Look at MAN's history. Is he always bound to destroy himself and others around him?"

Ian turned, sized me up and down but kept walking. He reached his table, gathered his belongings rhythmically, and left.

The pack of writers continued to talk amongst themselves. A few giggled nervously. Not a word was said about Ian.

I turned to the woman now by my side and introduced myself. "I'm Fred."

"I'm Mayday," she said. I didn't comment on her name, then, though I wanted to. I wanted to know what motivated someone to call themselves that. I doubted the name had been anyone else's choice.

"I saw your book Soul Pain Be Gone on the display. I like the title. It's like a mantra. I've been repeating it over and over in my mind since I came in."

"Thanks. I want to make a story group, and I don't want a booth outside. I want to have a corner in here. I love to hear people's personal soul stories."

"Why don't you leave this place, get your own and call it Pain's Corner?" I had a feeling it was a bad idea. Who would join a group called Pain's Corner? No one wanted pain. But I'm the one who suggested it. Why exactly I don't know.

And she agreed. She said it was something about the way I had taken Ian seriously. Something about the way I stood up for the underdog who seemed to not enjoy being the center of such attention. She liked me immediately, she told me later, and she felt like she knew me.

Mayday met new people every day. It was normal for her to strike up conversations with complete strangers. But she had very few friends. They could be counted on two fingers. I didn't know then that I would be the third. Yes, I had stood up for Ian, and she was going to keep me.

"If I make the group will you join?" she asked.

"Yes."

"Okay, and you can help me run it."

And with that, she turned, went to her table, pulled out a notepaper and in large black letters wrote:

DO YOU JUST WANT TO HANG OUT, GET ADVICE, ASK A QUESTION OR JUST VENT?

COME SHARE WITH US AT PAIN'S CORNER.
BE FUNNY, BE CRABBY, BE SILLY, BE SAD.
IT'S ALL GOOD. WE'LL MAKE YOU SMILE OR
CRACK YOU UP, THROUGH ACCEPTANCE
AND FRIENDSHIP, MAYBE EVEN SOME WIT.
For more information speak to Mayday.

I followed her and said in her ear: "Wait. Find the location first, before you start inviting everyone to join."

"Oh, don't worry, it'll all work out. I always do things backwards."

3

My name is Fred, and I am a helper.

We are just friends and spend a lot of time having coffee, talking on the phone, emailing and texting back and forth. I only meet with her on Sunday nights when Astrid goes to visit her mother.

Mayday is cute. She's refreshing. She is different from other people, and that makes her interesting. Mostly she is intriguing to me because we are so very different. I love her as my friend, and only a friend, as I've mentioned before. And she too has never showed me a sign of wanting anything more. I even talked to Astrid about her and she didn't say anything. She didn't object. After my almost-cheating fiasco a few years back, she knows I would never cheat again. But it wasn't really... I only let another woman in a bar please me with her hand... I didn't go to bed with her. And I was drunk. I would never do it again. Astrid knows that.

Astrid doesn't know that I speak with Mayday every night. I'm not sure why I didn't tell her; Astrid and I are close.

I felt sorry for Mayday, watching her struggle to build that loft, little house, shed, call it what you May. It was a room-like structure in her back yard. I watched for months on end as she tried to build it by herself. It was a disaster. She looked like a fool and I started to feel guilty about knowing how to do it and not helping her. I don't like getting involved in people's business. Each person has their own dream and their own struggle and their own nonsense wishes, and they should learn how to do it themselves as I have learned to do things myself. Mayday didn't know that I actually knew the ins and outs of construction, but she kept asking for help anyway. She begged, actually, and I always said no. Finally, one day, she called to tell me that she had built it and I was to go over and have a look.

When I went there I saw a mess. It was silly looking, and it was all pink. She had said she liked pink. Never did this woman call a bluff. It would have been better if she had. And I knew that dozens of people would be arriving within the next few weeks.

Well, as a professional architect I knew this little shed would collapse on them all. At the very least they would leave this place laughing at her. It was silly.

So I gave in. I gave up my rule to not get involved in people's business and I helped. In fact, I built the whole darn thing with her assisting me a little. She brought the hammer and the screws. The bigger pieces I fetched myself. And I did everything else too. She should have watched more closely and learned more. Alas, she is not a fast learner.

When I was done she thanked me a hundred times. She offered me a copy of her book. She offered me music to listen to. She offered me meals. I always refused. I didn't do it because I wanted anything in return. I just decided that she was trying so hard I might as well help. It was pathetic and I liked her as a person. Perhaps it was the difference between us. Perhaps it was that she shared the same birthday as my mother. I told Mayday she had said thank you enough times, and she was very welcome. She didn't need to thank me again.

She let me paint it grey, said not a word when she watched me do it. I knew she liked pink but there was no way I would use that silly color on anything I made.

4

My name is Fred, and I have felt pain.

I am a private man. I like an ordered life, above all, one that is responsible. Now forty years old, I am through with risk-taking. I have given up searching for hope. Humanity is evil. There is no hope for Man. God does not exist. After my mother died, I read every spiritual book there was trying to find out if there was a God and an afterlife, and above all, if any of that nonsense about Jesus is true. It isn't. I have seen countless of documentaries which prove that the myth of the Messiah is all created, that cultures of the past all thought they had a messiah in their midst. When, in fact, they didn't.

My mother died in suffering. She had diabetes, and they had had to cut off both her legs in the end. I loved my mother. I did everything I could to help her. I was there with her every day. I was there when she came back from the operating table without legs. It was unbearable to watch. Pain. I can't stand it. And it comes with everything it seems. My mother died when I was thirty-four years old. For six years I scoured the earth looking for the existence of a soul. Being an independent architect had its privileges. I was free to work when I wanted, accept the projects that interested me. And so, when an opportunity arose to work on a church or a mosque, I took it. I was there when they built those things that are said to house belief. So it wasn't that I didn't try to find meaning. I did. And there was absolutely nothing there, nothing but endless amounts of human pain and then the unknown, the nothing. The darkness.

Over and over life has disappointed me. Many years ago, I had a wife named Penelope. She wanted children. There was no way I was going to bring children into this painful world without hope. Since there is no hope for man, why make children?

Penelope just couldn't understand that. So we agreed to get a divorce. I adored her, a French Goddess—she was feisty and beautiful and told me exactly where to put it when I got out of line. She had her own opinions and did as she pleased. My kind of woman. But she caused so much pain.

When I told her that there was no way I was going to propagate, she said she was ready for a divorce. And I agreed. A divorce would be the best thing. We had different goals in life. We should go our own way.

It took one day to get the divorce. Six years of marriage, and it was over in one day. For months I roamed the streets and cried. I was sure she would come back. She would change her mind sooner or later. How could she choose unborn children over me? It was impossible. She loved me. I knew it. She would regret her choice, kids over me. Even if she never came back, she wouldn't be happy.

A year passed. Penelope had still not returned. Apparently she had a new boyfriend. I was still alone. And then I met Astrid. She was nice. She was my friend. She was polite and respectful. She didn't yell or chase me with a broom like Penelope did when I had too much to drink.

I have been with Astrid now for eight years. I made the wise choice to stick with her. For the most part, life has been calm and easy. Mayday made fun of her once saying she had a man's name. It was rough, she said, cold. But to me it's fine. Astrid has always been kind to me, and I like her, care about her even. She has done nothing to disrupt my life, doesn't interfere when I have work to do.

I never thought I would come across someone who would mock the choices I made in my life.

"Why are you with her?"

"Because I am."

"Why have you been with her for eight years?"

"Because there was no reason to leave."

"What kind of reason is that to stay with someone?"

"What?"

"Well, if someone ever asks me why I've been with someone for so many years, I'd like to say 'because I love him, because I could never imagine my life without him, because he makes my heart melt, because he is my soul mate, because I adore him, because he makes me fly.' There are so many reasons why you can be with someone, but not 'because there was no reason to leave.' I would die from pain if someone was with me just because there was no reason to leave."

Mayday is a witch.

5

My name is Fred, and I am a dream.

"I had a dream about you," she says suddenly one day, meddling with our beautiful, platonic friendship. "It was tingling and bright, like electricity."

"So, what was the dream?" I ask. "Was I a light bulb?"

"No, I decided to get into bed and read a new book I took out from the library. And as I was in bed I began to think about truth and how if I died tomorrow I would regret not telling it. Why? Because it's beautiful. It has energy, something refreshing, relaxing, like home. It calms the soul. And mine has been in turmoil lately, mostly because of guilt and shock. Guilt because I had two dreams about you. The second one I told you about right away because I was so worried, and I thought, what if something happens to him and I didn't tell him to be careful. So, I said to myself, to hell with pride and shame, tell him to be careful.

"So, I waited a couple of hours, suffering all morning, and I told you about the dream about your mangled feet. It was true.

"A week before though, I had had another dream, a beautiful dream, nothing vulgar about it, just magic. And I woke up stunned, incomplete shock, and I went downstairs and told Betty, 'Oh my God, I just had a dream about a friend of mine. I don't think you understand...he's a friend of mine. We've been working together for a long time. We really are friends. But the dream was magic, full of light, light in human form, like nothing I've ever seen before.'

"I decided 'there is no way I'm telling him such nonsense. I will swallow it.' I told Slone a day later, and he said it's just a dream.

"But now I understand, from way back when, why I trusted you—and have to tell you: You're light, Fred. You are light. You didn't know.

"I saw it when you spoke up for Ian— a fine feeling of silver light. And I love the light. Something said, 'Yes, trust him.'

"So just like that man in the store, in the mall, who stopped me to define the meaning of love, I had to tell. 'Cause imagine dying tomorrow and not telling. That would be terrible. That would be a lie.

"I feel lighter for sharing it. Thank you and sweet dreams."

Then she leaves, and the dream travels in my mind, and takes on its own life. I want to know. What exactly did she dream about? And for no particular reason, I want to know—the details. All the details.

6

My name is Fred, and I am a friend.

I hadn't been able to have female friends in years. Astrid wouldn't allow it after my bar slip-up. So when Mayday came along, I was happy. Finally I could have a female friend. Just a friend. That's all I wanted. Why, then, Mayday keeps asking, did I never mention Astrid?

"I don't know. There wasn't a need to."

"How can you be with someone so many years, and spend every night talking with me and not mention someone you are committed to?"

"I don't know. I didn't see the need to mention her."

"I would be upset if my boyfriend didn't mention me to another woman. I would be upset if my boyfriend thought there wasn't a need to mention me. The very first thing I do when I meet someone is mention whether I have a boyfriend or not. I slip him into the conversation so that the other person knows I am taken. So that they know what to expect from me. By not mentioning her, it shows that you wanted me to believe you were single. And when I asked you specifically if you had a girlfriend, you said you have four wives."

"You have a good memory."

"Yes, I have a photographic memory for words. I remember your exact words. You said you had four wives. If you didn't want this to continue all you had to do right then and there is tell me you had a girlfriend. Why didn't you tell me?"

"Because I thought I had mentioned her in the past and you knew."

"But I thought that since you had not mentioned her in three hundred and sixty five days, she was no longer there. Lots of people break up. I thought you had broken up."

"I just wanted a friend. I hadn't had a female friend in years. I missed having a female friend who didn't want me physically. I could never have a female friend because they all ended up falling in love and wanting to sleep with me."

"You wanted me. That is why you didn't mention your girlfriend. Do you love her?"

"I love you."

7

My name is Fred, and I am a cheater.

I swore to Astrid I would never cheat again. But this isn't really cheating. Mayday has never let me touch her. She lets me watch her and listen and imagine, but she said I am never to touch her as long as I'm with Astrid. She said she is queen and does not share—will never share a man.

I make fun of her. Queen, I call her, but she won't change her mind. I call her every day, many, many times a day. I email her and text her, and sometimes I meet her for coffee, but I still can't touch her. She has seen all of me, and I have seen all of her, and I can't get her out of my mind. She is there when I am eating with Astrid. She is there when I am working on my book. She is there when I am taking a shower. And I have never touched her. Maybe if I touch her I'll be able to get her out of my mind. Maybe this is all an obsession because I have not touched her. Am I attracted to her? Yes, enormously. I am always turned on. I feel young again. I feel revived. But she is driving me crazy. This is all driving me crazy. I have to find a solution. I must understand. When I understand I will be able to cope.

"You are cheating," Mayday says to me.

"I'm not cheating. You are not real. I have not touched you."

"I am real. You have felt my soul, looked into my eyes, seen me smile and laugh, exchanged ideas and thoughts, had arguments with me. I am real."

"You are not real. I don't know what you feel like. Maybe I won't like the way you feel."

"Because you do not touch something it doesn't make it less real. I cannot touch God, and He is real."

"You are a fairy, and I have imagined you. Maybe you are an illusion."

"How can you say I'm not real? You have met me dozens of times. You have felt me in your soul."

"There is no such thing as a soul."

"Okay, you have felt me in your soul which doesn't exist."

"Alright, maybe you are real, but maybe you are just an illusion. I don't know for sure. I have not touched you and therefore do not know you."

"Do you feel guilty about cheating on Astrid with me? I feel sick about doing this. I said I'd never be the other woman ever again in my life. It makes me ill."

"I'm not cheating. What we have is nothing. We have not touched."

"So cheating is only touching? When I was little, a group of us used to ask each other the question: 'What would you prefer, your husband to fall in love with another woman or for him to just sleep with another woman once, just for sex?' We all answered we would prefer our husband to just sleep with another woman once and be over with it. If he fell in love with another woman, it would hurt like hell. And love doesn't go away easily."

8

My name is Fred, and I am obsessed.

I see sex everywhere, in artwork, in clothing, in a religious structure, a boat, a shoe, a mathematics book (I plan to include models of gorgeous women in mine), in regular movies, and in every thought. Women are beautiful. Passion is beautiful. Mayday says I am obsessed with sex because it is intrinsic to my character, that I will only ever be truly happy if I have sex with a suitable partner. She says it is not normal that I haven't slept with Astrid in two years.

"It's normal," I tell her. "Sex in every relationship subsides after the first six months."

"That's not true. I was in a relationship for two years and it never got boring. Maybe you guys are just not a fit. Maybe you have no creative energy."

"No, stupee. We get along. We like each other and are friends. After eight years it is normal that we don't have sex."

"Do you sleep together every night, in the same bed?"

"Yes."

"Does she kiss you goodbye when she leaves?"

"Yes."

"Does she tell you she loves you?"

"Yes."

"What do you answer?

"What?"

"What do you answer when she tells you she loves you? Do you say 'me too'?"

"Yes."

"So, you tell her you love her, and then you come and tell me you love me."

I don't know what to tell her anymore. She's trapped me. Again.

"Say you love Astrid."

"I love you."

"Say you love her."

"I love you."

"Say, 'I love Astrid.' Say it."

"I love you."

"Close your eyes."

"What?"

"Close your eyes and see me."

"I want to leave them open."

"Do you see my hands going up?"

"You haven't moved them."

"See with your soul. Do you feel my hands moving up? Look at my eyes now, only my eyes and feel my arms rising."

"Okay." Her hands are still by her side.

"Do you feel the wind moving around us?"

"What are you doing?"

"Feel it, feel the wind moving around us."

"Okay."

"Feel the world moving around us. Feel things changing. Feel things happening. The energy is moving. Uuuhhhh," she groans.

"What are you doing to me?"

"Nothing."

She was doing something. I felt it. My heart was beating fast.

9

My name is Fred, and I am a drunk.

She wanted to invite anyone and everyone to spend all hours of the day to the shed, and I didn't object. It was after all hers. She said it was mine too because it had been my idea. I told her I didn't want it. It was only hers.

She gave me the key, and after a month, the place was rocking. People were coming in and out all day, laughing, joking, sharing their ideas and stories and pain.

And then one day I got drunk. Mayday was not there. Only one other guy was there. His name was

Paul. He wasn't speaking. He was sitting in the corner, watching. Or pretending to be illustrating. Whichever you prefer.

He told her later that I was totally off the wall and that if I didn't leave he wouldn't return. She needed him for her book. She couldn't illustrate. But she told him I was her friend. She never told me this. I found this out later through the grapevine, and her diary, which lay open in front of me as I was cleaning up one day. I would never deliberately intrude on her privacy, but it was there, right in front of me, and my eyes grasped the words. She ditched him. For me.

She had my mother's birthday.

10

My name is Fred, and I am a traitor.

She pushed me and pushed me. She did not listen. I told her not to call my house phone. Only my cell. She did not understand. She did not respect my wishes. What would happen if I moved in with her, married her? She would not listen to my wishes.

I betrayed her. I was cold and I knew it. I had no choice. She gave me no choice. Mayday is crazy. I do not trust her. How could she do that? How could she call my house and possibly harm me? There is a difference between hurt and harm. You can hurt someone over and over. But to harm someone is irreversible. And unforgettable. You can never put your guard down again.

She said she felt betrayed. How could I tell her I loved her over and over again and then speak to her like she was a stranger? How could I?

Astrid was watching me. She was by the phone, that is how. I had no choice. My suitcase had been placed by the door, and I had to make a decision. Stay with safe, someone I knew, or go with wild and unforeseeable. Unpredictable. Dangerous and delicious. But she was not safe. She would leave me one day. I trusted her with money but not with sex and love. She would stop loving me.

I stayed.

Astrid never stopped mentioning her.

11

My name is Fred, and I am honorable.

I have lost all my jobs. There are no more contracts to be found. I am forty years old and no one seems to want to hire me. I am smart, Mayday says. But how can I find a job if I spend my day and night thinking about her, calling her, writing to her, meeting with her. She is on my mind and nothing else.

"Don't you feel guilty taking money from Astrid and being with me?" she asks.

"Yes, very," I answer.

"Doesn't it make more sense to take money from me, then?"

"I can't do it."

"Why not?"

"I cannot take money from you."

"Why not?"

"Because of your father." Mayday lives with her father. She pays all the bills and takes care of him. He got Alzheimer's the year Mayday turned sixteen. She has been caring for him for ten years now. She loves him.

12

My name is Fred, and I am compassionate.

I found a bird and brought it home. It was a little bird, and it was dying. I took care of it, tried to restore it, but it died anyway. I cried.

I can never have pets again.

13

My name is Fred, and I pray to God.

I don't believe in God. I'm sure He doesn't exist. I know the soul does not exist. I know they are all human fabrications, myths. But I pray sometimes. Rodney's child was sick and Mayday asked me to pray. I did. She never asked how I could pray to God if I believe that He doesn't exist.

Sometimes I say 'Good Lord.' Like one time I was suffering when she decided not to talk to me because I had told her I had slept with Astrid. Mayday didn't answer my calls and refused to see me for four weeks. I suffered. I was in pain. I have never felt such pain before in my life. I thought I couldn't breathe. Every day was a nightmare. Astrid asked me what was wrong. I said nothing. I sent Mayday text messages without thinking of what I was writing. I really couldn't breathe.

I swore for almost a month that it was untrue. I did not sleep with Astrid. I swore to my mother's grave, and she finally believed me. I loved my mother. I would not desecrate her.

14

My name is Fred, and I am faithless.

She says anyone who has no faith has only fear. That is why I cannot make a decision. She has promised me the world. Everything she has and is, that is. The world, her, a life like no other. A life where people really and truly love each other, a life of exploring. She says she wants to explore the world with me, go to different countries and find God. I told her I have already done that and there is no God. I told her I don't want to do that and she will have to do it alone. She says we will do it together.

15

My name is Fred, and I am real.

And she is a fairy in a box. She is a beautiful, magical fairy. She consoles and feeds. She kills my boredom. She adds spice and interest in my life. I want to die with her. I do not want to live with her. But I want to keep her. She is not worth the effort of making change. She is not trustworthy as she has changed so many men. She discards them like flies. She is like a spider gulping them up, and then they are gone, their lives destroyed. And then she haunts them. I am smart enough to know this. She says that is how she kills.

"What?" I say. "Explain. How do you kill?"

"I just leave them. That is death."

"How is that death?"

"Because I have a high tolerance for pain, and they think I will never leave, but I do. I leave them. And when I leave I am happy to be leaving. I feel fulfilled and happy."

"So it is revenge for you."

"No, it is not revenge. It is just my time to leave. I have had enough."

"Enough of what?"

"I have had enough of being mistreated. I have a high tolerance, but eventually I've had it. And I never look back."

"I bet you they don't even want you back."

"Yes, they do."

"You are a maneater."

"No, I'm kind. They do it to themselves."

16

I am a ghost ship.

I wonder whether the ghost ship is going anywhere or whether it is going to sink in the middle of the Atlantic Ocean. It's a dark scary full moon night, and the ocean seems to be hungry for lost ships.

17

I am a pimp.

She called me a pimp. I think I am just a man who is afraid of making a decision. She thinks I'm a pimp. I said yes, go ahead and date and we'll see what happens.

It has been one year and a half since the actual love part of this thing started. Mayday has given me plenty of time to decide, and all the facts. I have asked for every detail of every possible scenario. She has answered and answered, and I love her for doing so. But what she asks is illogical. I cannot budge.

She says she wants to start dating again. Not me. Other people.

The six months she gave me to think about it are up. And I say, yes, do it, and we'll see what happens.

She did it. And I almost died.

18

I have been robbed.

She took my words. She said my soul is in my words, and she has been waiting for it forever, and I will not give it. She said she decided to take them. She will put them in a book and keep them. On a silver platter. Her book is the silver platter. She will own them and eat them whenever she wants. She will inhale them. They are hers. She tricked me. She asked me for a story, and I simply answered. She had told me that she was writing a book and was collecting stories for the book, but I didn't actually believe she would use mine.

She should have known better. Those words were only for her. They are not for public consumption. She is a thief. She stole. Yes, I gave, but they were only for her. She violated me. She took without permission. I feel naked. I feel hurt. I feel betrayed. I don't want her anymore.

She does not to want me either. She says she is happy now; she has my words. She says she finally discovered that is where my soul lies. She says it is the perfect ending to a story.

She offered to change my name, but the words she will keep.

I threatened her with the police. I said it was identity theft. She said, "How is that identity theft when I'm not stealing your identity?" She was only taking the words that I gave her. I gave them to her, she said. She offered to change my name, and then bid me goodbye. I have not heard from her since.

She took a part of me and left. And now here I am, alone, staring at the walls. They are empty. There is no soul like she described it. I feel naked.

Exposed. And the world has no meaning. It makes no sense. But then, what is the sense of the word "sense"?

19

I am a dead end.

Mayday confirmed she doesn't want to continue. She doesn't care if we ever meet again. She's not sure if she loves me anymore, but she knows that she doesn't want anything more from me. She said even if I left Astrid she wouldn't want me. She said she never wants to be with me.

As for me, I still love her, but I don't want to be with her. She is too risky. She is lovely, but I need safe. I need someone who I know will stay with me forever. Sex and passion are a high price to pay for safety.

Besides, how could I ever trust her knowing she doesn't respect my wishes? She said she is not a puppy and will do as she pleases.

She said thank you for the gift of the words; she will keep them. I never intended for her to really use them. She asked me for a story, and I gave it. I never believed she would actually put it in her book. The woman never bluffs.

I suspect she never wants to meet with me again because she got to the ending of her story. She turned out to be a taker of words, and I turned out to be the end.

She says she brought me back to life but that I am a dead end. She took my words. I suspect she needs me for nothing else.

20

I am a man.

And she is a maneater. Did she eat me? Yes, I believe so. She ate my soul, the very thing she wanted. Does that then make her a souleater? Does that then make me a soul? That's her line of thinking. It's become infectious. She's gotten into my mind.

I still have Astrid, so do not cry for me. Mayday will come back begging. Maybe not. I have never been big on knowing. What did I find out from this experience? Nothing. That nothing is for sure. And man— including woman, of course,—is evil.

From May

You have sat there and consoled each other as to why it is a great thing that you have not had kids.

And now you can sit there and look at her, empty, and say, "Wow, you look great, dear. Your vulva isn't hanging—but I don't want to fuck you still. Your breasts are perfect, but I don't want to touch them still."

Like Homo Faber; the irony and the slap of life. You spend your whole life avoiding something, and then you realize it's empty...all that beauty is empty—because it has no context.

I'm listening to the song *I'm not in love* by CC. It's beautiful and makes me think love is the beginning and the end and ultimate state of grace.

Notice how people run from it when it's happening, and then, in the future, they try to retrieve and duplicate that very same feeling...for how extraordinary it was.

Love forever,
May
June 19th

The End

I don't think these talks have helped me much.
I have been here for twenty weeks. A long time.
Everyone is starting to smell like fish.

May no longer writes to me or talks to me. She
wrote to me once and asked me if I ever loved her.
I sent her the link to the song *I will always love you* by
Whitney Houston. A beautiful song. Perhaps she
wanted words. More words. That's all I had to
offer. But it's true, I will always love her.

This place is pointless. And I am not the same
man. But I will remain with Astrid. She is safe.

I don't know what Mayday means about vulvas and things. I don't care about them anymore. Love, what is that anyway?

67